FOLK

For Miles and Jude

First edition published by Holders Hill Publishing in 2021
Second edition published by Holders Hill publishing in 2022

Copyright © Nathan Holder, 2021

A Cataloguing-in-Publication catalogue record for this book is available from the British Library

ISBN 978-1-7395839-2-7

www.thewhybooks.co.uk

Book layout and illustration by Charity Russell
www.charityrussell.com

Where Are All The Instruments?
European Orchestra

Nathan Holder
Illustrated by Charity Russell

HOLDERS HILL

'Where are all our instruments?'
cried the musicians.
'They're all gone!'

'I can see a bassoon under the slide!' said Phoebe.
'It's bigger than a clarinet, and it has more keys.'

Back on land, Olivia made another discovery. 'I've found this! It's like a violin, but bigger. It's called a viola,' she said.

After a short walk, they arrived at the wildlife sanctuary.
'Wow! This is even bigger than a cello!' said Olivia.
'It's called a double bass.'

'What are those?' pointed Phoebe.
'These big drums are called timpani,' said Zaki. 'They're really loud!'

Instruments

Bassoon

Oboe

Clarinet

Piano

Timpani

Cello

Double Bass

Viola

Violin

Questions And Answers

Can you find all of the hidden instruments?

Can you find the hidden alien?

What is your favourite instrument?

Lightning Source UK Ltd.
Milton Keynes UK
UKHW050319030323
417931UK00004B/92